1997 Barnes & Noble Books

ISBN 0-76070-456-2

Printed and bound in the United States of America

97 98 99 00 M 9 8 7 6 5 4 3 2 1

QF

# Cookies and Crutches

## JUDY DELTON

*Illustrated by Alan Tiegreen*

A YOUNG YEARLING BOOK

For Dyana Peters,
who has Pee Wee Scouts of her own

# Contents

# CHAPTER 1

# Three O'clock at Last

Molly Duff watched the clock.

The big black minute hand dropped, boing, boing, boing.

One minute at a time.

To get to three o'clock, it had to climb, chug, chug, chug.

At three o'clock the bell would ring.

The Pee Wee Scouts from first grade would run out of the room and down the stairs. They were in Troop 23.

Clop, clop, clop.

Tuesday was their meeting day.

1

Molly could not wait.

Today Mrs. Peters would show them how to bake cookies.

Mmm. Molly felt hungry thinking about it.

She could not sit still in her seat on Tuesdays.

She pretended to think very hard about her spelling words.

She squinted and said, "Pig: p-i-g."

But she was not thinking about *pig*.

She was thinking about Scouts and cookies.

Molly knew how to spell.

She could spell *pig* without thinking at all.

Spelling was easy.

"Mary Beth, spell *home*," said Mrs. Lane.

Mary Beth Kelly was passing a note to Sonny Betz.

Mrs. Lane watched for people who passed notes.

Mary Beth turned red.
She was not good at spelling.
"Spell *home*," Mrs. Lane said again.

"Home-comb," said Molly to herself.
"Let's go to Scouts!"

Mrs. Lane looked as if she wanted to leave too.

She spelled *home* for Mary Beth.

"Keep your eyes on your spelling, Mary Beth," said Mrs. Lane.

"Yes, Mrs. Lane," said Mary Beth.

Molly looked at the clock. Chug, chug, chug.

The big hand was climbing to three.

"Home," said Mrs. Lane. "It is almost time to go home!"

Sonny Betz waved his hand.

"Not for us!" he said.

"It is Tuesday. We have Scouts on Tuesday."

4

"Dear me, I forgot!" said Mrs. Lane.

Teachers were not supposed to forget, thought Molly.

That was a teacher's job. To remember everything.

It was good that the first graders remembered it was Tuesday.

Remembered it was Scout day.

Or else Mrs. Peters would be all alone with her cookies.

Gobble, gobble, gobble.

Mrs. Peters would eat all the cookies herself!

Dozens and dozens of cookies!

Molly laughed into her speller thinking about it.

The minute hand was still climbing. Chug, chug, chug.

"Row One, get your coats," said Mrs. Lane.

Row One raced to the back of the room.

"Row Two is noisy," said Mrs. Lane. "I will call on Row Three because they are quiet."

Row Three raced to the back of the room.

Molly sat up straight. She sat very very still. She was in Row Two.

Mrs. Lane looked at Molly.

"Row Two," she said.

Row Two got their coats.

Some of the children got in line.

Then Mrs. Lane called, "Pee Wee Scouts, line up!"

\* \* \*

6

The minute hand climbed its last minute.
It was on the twelve.
The bell rang, BRRRING!

Molly covered her ears. The bell was right outside the first-grade door!
The lines marched out of the room.
It was time for Pee Wee Scouts at last!
It was time to learn how to bake cookies.

# CHAPTER 2

# Raw Dough!

Troop 23 ran all the way down the stairs.
The school bus waited near the door.
Molly wanted to get there first.
She squeezed ahead of Mary Beth Kelly.
Then she squeezed ahead of Sonny Betz.
But Rachel Myers was there first.
She was in the other first grade.

"That's not fair," said Molly. "Your room is closer to the door."
"I can run faster," said Rachel.

9

"I've got my running shoes on."

Molly looked at Rachel's running shoes. Everybody had some.

Everybody but Molly.

Molly's mother said running shoes were not school shoes.

"A hex on your running shoes," said Molly, crossing her eyes.

Molly said that when she was mad.

It made her feel better.

It scared some people.

They thought she might really put a hex on them.

But she couldn't.

A hex was not a real thing.

The Scouts got on the school bus.

They got off at Mrs. Peters's house.

Mrs. Peters was waiting at the door.

"We'll meet in the kitchen today," she said.

The Scouts followed her one by one.

She had bowls and spoons out.
She had flour and butter and sugar.
"Umm," said Molly, rubbing her stomach.

Everyone stood around the table.
They all wanted to be in front.
They all wanted to see.
Mostly, they all wanted a cookie!

Mrs. Peters smiled.
She was friendly and kind.
She was a good troop leader.

"Before we begin, does anyone have a good deed to report?" Mrs. Peters asked the Scouts.

"I helped my grandma wash her windows this week," said Sonny Betz.

"Good!" said Mrs. Peters.

"I carried three bags of groceries for the lady next door," said Roger White.

"Wonderful," said Mrs. Peters. "You've been real Pee Wees this week. Today, I will show you how to make easy cookies.

"To earn your cookie badge, you must bake cookies yourself.

"You must bake them at home and bring one to me.

"I will see if you earn the badge.

"Your parents must not help.

"But they must know you are using the stove.

"And they must write a note saying you baked them yourselves.

"Do you all understand what to do?"

The Scouts nodded.

All except Roger White.

"Baking cookies is for girls," he said.

"It is not," said Sonny Betz.

"Sissy!" said Roger. "Mama's boy!"

Lots of people thought Sonny was a sissy.

His mother still walked to school with him every morning.

She met him after school too.

Mrs. Peters held up her hand.

"Do you like to eat, Roger?" she said.

Roger nodded.

"If boys can eat, boys can cook," she said. "Baking and cooking are for everyone."

"Yeah!" shouted Sonny. "I told you, creep!"

Mrs. Peters began to measure flour.

She explained the measuring cups.

And the measuring spoons.

She mixed the butter and sugar.

She put in eggs.

She put in flour.

She mixed it all up.

At the end she put in chocolate chips and nuts.

"Umm," said Molly and Mary Beth together.

"I could eat them right now. Before they are baked," said Rachel.

Roger made gagging noises.

"You can't eat raw flour," he said. "Yuck!"

"And raw eggs," said Molly. "Right out of a chicken!"

"It's good!" said Rachel. "I could eat that whole bowl of dough right now!"

Now everyone was making gagging sounds.

Mrs. Peters had to hold her hand up again.

She showed the Scouts how to scoop the dough with a teaspoon and put it on

the pan. When the pan was full, she put it into the oven.

"Now!" she said. "We put the timer on for twelve minutes. While we wait, we will sing our Pee Wee Scout song!"

Troop 23 got into a circle.

Mrs. Peters washed her hands at the sink.

Everybody sang.

## Pee Wee Song

(to the tune of
"Old MacDonald Had a Farm")

Scouts are helpers, Scouts have fun,
Pee Wee, Pee Wee Scouts!
We sing and play when work is done,
Pee Wee, Pee Wee Scouts!

With a good deed here,
And an errand there,
Here a hand, there a hand,
Everywhere a good hand.

Scouts are helpers, Scouts have fun,
Pee Wee, Pee Wee Scouts!

While the Scouts sang, they sniffed the air.

The cookies smelled wonderful, baking.

# CHAPTER 3

# Root Beer to the Rescue

**W**hen the cookies were done, Mrs. Peters gave one to each Scout.

"Umm," said Molly. "These are good cookies!"

The cookies were warm and soft.

The chocolate chips were melted and ran down the Scouts' fingers.

"See if you can make good cookies too," said Mrs. Peters.

"Be sure your mother is home. Be careful when you use the stove."

Mrs. Peters passed out papers.
They were recipes for how to make the cookies.

~~~~~~~~~~~~~~~~~~~~~~~~~~~~~~~~~~~~~~~~~~~

 **Pee Wee Cookies**

3/4 cup brown sugar
3/4 cup white sugar
1 cup butter
2 eggs
2 tsp. vanilla

Mix well.

Then add: 1 tsp. baking soda
1 tsp. salt

2 cups flour
1 cup oatmeal
2 cups cornflakes
1 pkg. chocolate chips (8 oz.)
1/2 cup nuts

Drop small spoonfuls of dough on greased cookie sheet.
Bake at 350 degrees for 12 minutes.

~~~~~~~~~~~~~~~~~~~~~~~~~~~~~~~~~~

"Let's make cookies together, at my house," Mary Beth said to Molly.

"Can we make cookies together?" asked Molly.

"Yes," said Mrs. Peters. "You can work together."

It was time for Scouts to end.
Everyone said the Pee Wee Pledge.

## 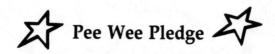 Pee Wee Pledge

We love our country
And our home,
Our school and neighbors too.

As Pee Wee Scouts
We pledge our best
In everything we do.

Then they put their coats on to leave.

"Let's make our cookies now," said Mary Beth on the way home.

"No, they'll be stale by next Tuesday," said Molly. "Let's make them Monday after school."

The next day was Wednesday. During recess Mary Beth walked up to Sonny.

"We're making our cookies together," she told him.

"We are too," said Sonny. "Aren't we, Roger?"

"I s'pose," said Roger.

He was thinking of how warm and soft those cookies were.

He remembered that Mrs. Peters said if boys could eat, boys could cook.

It made sense.

At three o'clock the next Monday the girls hurried to Mary Beth's house.

When they got there, Mary Beth's mother had chocolate chips ready.

She had flour and sugar and eggs out.

"The oven is on," Mrs. Kelly said. "I'll be upstairs. Call me if you need me."

"We will," said Mary Beth.

Molly took the paper out of her pocket.
It had the cookie recipe on it.
"Measure the flour," she said.
Mary Beth measured the flour.
She poured it into the bowl.
Molly measured the butter into another bowl.
She put an egg in too.
They both did just what it said on the paper.
First Mary Beth stirred it, and then Molly.
"There is something the matter," said Mary Beth.
Molly looked into the bowl.
"It should be brown," said Mary Beth. "Mrs. Peters's cookies were brown."
"Maybe the chips will make it brown," said Molly.

She dumped the chips in.

It still was not brown.

It was almost white, like flour.

"We need something brown," said Mary Beth, opening the refrigerator.

She reached for a bottle of root beer. It was brown.

"Let's put some of this in," she said.

Molly looked doubtful. It was brown, though.

And the cookie dough did look too white.

She poured some of the root beer into the batter.

Fizzzzz!

Little bubbles were all over.

Molly stirred it.

"It's too runny now," she said. "We need something to make it thick."

Mary Beth looked in the cupboard. She reached for a package of something that had a brown picture on the box.

"What does this say?" she asked.

"Gravy mix," read Molly. "That's good! My mom uses it to make gravy thick when it's too runny. So it would make this thick too."

Mary Beth dumped the box of gravy mix into the cookie dough.

"Perfect!" said Molly. "It's real thick now."

"Thick and brown!" said Mary Beth. "It looks like Mrs. Peters's cookies."

"Now there is more dough," said Molly.

"But not enough chocolate chips!" added Mary Beth.

"I like lots of chocolate chips," said Molly.

"So do I," said Mary Beth. "That's the best part."

The girls looked in the cupboards and in the refrigerator. There were no more chips.

"We need something!" said Mary Beth, stamping her foot.

"These look like chips," said Molly, picking up a plastic bag.

"Dump them in!" said Mary Beth.

The girls stirred and stirred. Then they put the cookies on the pan one at a time, as Mrs. Peters had shown them.

"Terrific!" said Molly. "They look yummy!"

* * *

Mary Beth popped the pan into the oven.

She set the timer for twelve minutes.

"Now all we do is wait," she said. "Wait for our yummy yummy cookies."

# CHAPTER 4

# Baked Frisbees

"**W**ash the dishes when you're through," called Mary Beth's mother from upstairs.

The girls sighed. Cookies were more work than Mrs. Peters had said.

They washed the dishes and then went to Mary Beth's room to wait.

Pretty soon Mary Beth's mother called out, "What is that smell?"

The girls sniffed the air.

"It smells like turkey roasting," said Mrs. Kelly.

"Our cookies!" Molly shouted.

The cookies were not white now.

They were very very brown.

And they were huge.

"They look like hamburgers!" said Molly.

"But they smell like turkey!" said Mary Beth.

Mary Beth's mother came into the kitchen.

She picked up the gravy mix box.

"No wonder it smells like turkey!" she said.

"Why did you use this?"

"The cookies were runny," said Mary Beth.

"From the root beer," said Molly.

"Why did you use root beer?" asked Mary Beth's mother.

"To make them brown," said Molly.

"Baking makes them brown," said Mrs. Kelly.

"It sure does," said Mary Beth.

The girls took the cookies off the pan and put them on a plate.

"They look like giant Frisbees!" cried Mary Beth.

"Or flying saucers," said Molly. "We will never get a badge for these cookies."

"Let's taste one," said Mary Beth.

Mrs. Kelly had gone back upstairs.

Mary Beth took one bite.

She made a terrible face. She ran to the sink and spit it out.

"It's awful!" she said.

"And there is something hard in there."
Mary Beth took a drink of water. "Something real hard," she said.

Molly broke her cookie in half.

She saw little marble-like things inside.

"Yuck!" she said. "I'm not eating these things. They look like beans!"

"Now we won't get our badge," said Mary Beth.

She stamped her foot. She felt mad.

What a waste. They could not even eat the cookies.

"I better go home," said Molly, getting her coat on.

"Take your half of the cookies," said Mary Beth.

"No thanks!" cried Molly. "There's a hex on those cookies, and I didn't put it there!"

# CHAPTER 5

# Cookie Badges

On Tuesday almost everyone brought a cookie to the meeting.

Some looked like submarines.
Some looked like brown buttons.
Some looked like dog chewies.
But none looked like chocolate chip cookies.

"Today we will try again," said Mrs. Peters.

"Right here. I will not help.

"I will just watch.

"Put in only what it says on the paper."

"That was our mistake," whispered Sonny. "We put in too much other stuff."

"We did too," said Molly.

"I didn't," said Rachel in her running shoes.

"Then why were your cookies so yucky?" asked Roger.

"They weren't yucky," Rachel said. "They just didn't get done. I didn't bake them long enough."

"Dough-face," said Roger. "You're the girl who eats raw dough! Dough-face! Dough-face! Raw-cookie monster Rachel!"

Rachel stuck out her tongue at him.

Each Scout had his or her own bowl. They had their own measuring cups.

They had only the right cookie things.

Mrs. Peters watched them as they made their cookies.

She put them into the oven.

She set the timer.

This time all the cookies turned out.

Some were big and some were small.

Some were square and some were round.

Some were oblong.

But they all were soft and warm and had melted chocolate chips in them.

Each Scout gave Mrs. Peters a cookie to taste.

"Wonderful!" she said.

She passed out the cookie badges. The badges were shaped like big cookies. The Scouts pinned them onto their Scout kerchiefs. Then they ate their cookies while Mrs. Peters told them about plans for a skating party.

It was a special party. The Scouts were all supposed to bring their dads.

Everyone looked at Tim Noon.

He didn't have a dad.

Neither did Lisa Ronning or Sonny Betz.

"If you don't have a dad," Mrs. Peters was saying, "you can bring a brother, or an uncle, or even a friend."

"Yikes!" said Rachel. "I get to wear my new figure skates!"

Molly didn't have skates.

Mary Beth had some, but they were black.

Her big brother had outgrown them.

"You can always borrow skates, or rent skates if you don't have any," said Mrs. Peters.

"I have some, Mrs. Peters," called Rachel from across the room. "They are white figure skates. I won't have to borrow or rent any," she said.

"Fine, Rachel," said Mrs. Peters.

Rachel stood on her toes and made skating motions as if she were already on the ice.

"Show-off," muttered Roger. "I'll bet your skates are dumb."

"My skates are what the stars wear to

skate on TV," said Rachel with her hands on her hips.

"A hex on your skates," whispered Molly with her eyes crossed.

"And a hex on chocolate chip cookies," said Mary Beth, moaning. "I ate too many. I don't ever want to see a cookie again in my whole life!"

# CHAPTER 6

# Dainty Feet

The Pee Wee Scouts counted the days until the skating party. It was on a Saturday afternoon.

It was at the indoor skating rink downtown.

"A hex on school," said Molly Duff on Friday afternoon.

She glared at Mrs. Lane.

First grade was boring sometimes.

Molly knew how to read.

She knew how to spell.

What she didn't know how to do was skate.

They should teach skating in first grade, she thought.

That would be more sensible. Something she didn't know.

Something that was fun.

Chug, chug, chug. The big hand of the clock climbed to the three.

BRRRING! rang the bell at last.

The school day was over.

The skating party was almost here.

In the hall, Molly met Rachel.

She had on her running shoes.

She had on a lavender jacket.

Molly liked lavender. Her mother said it was too fancy a color for first grade.

"It's Ultrasuede," said Rachel when she saw Molly looking at her jacket.

Ultrasuede was very expensive.

No one in first grade had anything Ultrasuede, except Rachel. Rachel's family must have a lot of money, Molly thought.

Rachel turned up the collar on her jacket.

"My dad has figure skates too," said Rachel. "Black ones."


Black-schmack. Rachel's whole family probably were show-offs.

A hex on her father's black figure skates, thought Molly.

She would have to rent skates.

Her father would too.

Even Mary Beth had to rent skates, or wear her brother's black ones.


On Saturday afternoon the Pee Wee

Scouts met at the school. They wore their Pee Wee kerchiefs. Mrs. Peters got rides for the Scouts who needed them.

Rachel was there with her white figure skates.

They had white laces with blue pom-poms on them.

The blades were shiny. You could almost see your face in them, like a mirror. They had notches on the end to twirl with.

Her father had black skates. His blades were shiny too.

His black laces had red balls on them.

Just like figure skaters in the Ice Capades on TV.

Lisa Ronning was there with her uncle. He had a red tassel cap on.

He looked very young. Almost like a brother.

All the fathers and uncles and brothers were laughing together.

In the middle of all of the adults, there was one woman.

"Who is that?" whispered Molly to Mary Beth. "Why is she here?"

People were laughing, and pointing to Sonny.

"It's Sonny's mom!" said Mary Beth. "Sonny brought his *mom* instead of his dad."

"Mrs. Peters said you had to bring a *dad*," said Molly. "Or at least a brother or an uncle!"

Mary Beth nodded. She pulled on her new wool hat.

"Sonny does everything with his mom," she said.

Roger was poking Sonny, and saying,

"Sissy! Bringing your mom to a fathers' skating party!"

Roger was bent over now, laughing.

"My mom can skate," said Sonny. "She can probably skate better than your dad."

"Ha!" said Roger. "We'll see about that."

*     *     *

Roger began to worry about whether his dad could skate.

He wondered if he could skate himself.

He hadn't been skating for over a year.

He was in kindergarten the last time he was on the ice.

Everyone piled into cars.

All the men.

And all the Scouts.

And Mrs. Betz.

When they got to the indoor rink, Mrs. Peters had everyone's tickets ready.

The men went to a counter to rent skates.

The Scouts who did not have their own skates went to another counter, where they could rent children's sizes.

Molly and Mary Beth got in line to rent skates.

Rachel followed them, even though she had skates of her own.

She hung them around her neck by the laces.

The blue pom-poms were bouncing as she walked.

"Your feet are really big," she said to Molly.

"They are not," said Molly quickly.

"What size do you wear?" demanded Rachel.

"I can't remember," lied Molly.

"These are size ten," said Rachel proudly, pointing to her skates. "My mom says ten is a very small size for my age. She says I have dainty feet."

"Size please," said the man behind the counter.

Molly didn't stop to think. "Ten," she said.

"You don't wear ten," said Rachel, pouting.

"I do too," said Molly, taking the skates.

When Mary Beth had rented her skates, the three girls walked over to a bench. They sat down and began to unlace the skates. They put them on.

Mary Beth pulled hers on easily and laced them up.

Rachel pulled hers on carefully and laced them up.

The blades sparkled. The pom-poms danced.

She stood up on the ice in front of Molly and twirled.

*   *   *

Molly's skate wouldn't go on. And it was not white like Rachel's. It was gray. The blades were not like mirrors. They were dull.

She pulled and pulled.

She tugged and tugged.

"Those are too small!" whispered Mary Beth. "Why don't you get a bigger size?"

Molly did not want a bigger size.

She wanted the same size as Rachel.

She did not have big feet.

A hex on Rachel for saying so.

"My socks are too thick," said Molly. "I have to take them off."

She took her socks off and put them into her pocket.

Then she tried to pull the skates on again.

"Your feet are too big," said Rachel.

She stopped twirling and put her hands on her hips.

She stared at Molly's feet.

"They are not!" said Molly, pulling extra hard on the skate.

POP! It went on.

But it felt awful.

Molly's toes were bent. Maybe they were even broken!

Molly could not move one toe. She tried to lace up the skate. She had to pull the lace tightly to tie it.

She pulled and tugged on the other skate to get it on.

Finally it went pop! Her heel slid in. But just barely.

Now all ten toes felt as if they were bent in half.

How would she ever be able to stand up?

Both Rachel and Mary Beth were twirling on the ice.

They reached out their mittened hands to pull her up.

Oof! She was on her feet! The pain from her toes went all the way up her ankles.

"Come on then," said Rachel in her size-ten skates. "Let's skate together."

# CHAPTER 7

# Crutches

**M**olly was in the middle.

Rachel had hold of one arm, and Mary Beth had the other.

They skated along, pulling Molly with them.

After a little while Molly could not feel her feet at all.

They were numb!

Molly's dad came skating up to them.

His arms were out.

He wobbled from one side to the other.

His knees bent in, and then out.

"I'm not too good at this," he said, laughing.

Mary Beth's father came skating over to them.

He was better.

But not much better.

He slid toward them.

Crash! He bumped into a bench, and fell onto the ice!

Rachel's father came gliding toward them.

He was skating smoothly. Just like Rachel.

His blades flashed as he came to a stop.

Ice chips flew up where he stood.

Most of the dads were having trouble standing up.

They wobbled back and forth and fell onto the ice.

"Look at Roger and his dad!" cried Rachel. "They are bumping into everyone!"

Mrs. Peters was helping the fathers to their feet.

She was showing them how to put one foot ahead of the other.

She showed some of the Pee Wee Scouts how to stop.

"Look!" called Molly, pointing.

There, skating smoothly among all the wobbling dads, was Mrs. Betz.

In and out, in and out.

Then she skated arm in arm with Sonny.

Then she skated backward.

And then, while everyone watched, Mrs. Betz skated with both arms out and one leg out in back of her. Just like the skaters on TV!

All the dads began to clap. Mrs. Betz bowed and waved.

"See?" said Sonny as he whizzed by Roger. "What did I tell you? I told you my mom could skate better than your dad!"

Roger turned red. He couldn't call Sonny a sissy now.

He and his mother could outskate them all!

"Hex, hex, hex," called Molly to Sonny and his mom.

Her feet were aching. She felt awful.

"Try this!" said Rachel, skating with one leg out in front of her.

Molly tried it and toppled over sideways.

"Come on, Molly!" they called. "You're no fun today!"

Molly got to her feet.

She closed her eyes in pain, and tried again to put one leg out in front of her. It did not work.

She turned her ankle and fell on the ice.

"I can't walk!" she said, trying to get to her feet.

When her father pulled her up, she could not stand on her sore ankle.

"It's broken!" she cried.

Everyone ran to help.

They carried Molly to the bench.

Mrs. Peters showed them how to make a stretcher with a coat, and they took her to the car.

Molly's father began to take her skates off.

Molly cried in pain.

"Let's wait," said Mrs. Peters, who always took charge. "It is best not to disturb a patient."

Molly could not believe what was happening to her.

Her father's car was taking her to the hospital!

Was her ankle really broken?

She should not have lied about her skate size.

A hex on size ten!

At the hospital everyone got out.

They followed the coat-stretcher.

It looked like a parade.

In the emergency room a nurse X-rayed Molly's ankle.

The doctor came in and felt Molly's bones.

He looked at the X rays.

"It is not broken," he said. "Just sprained. You have a sprained ankle, Molly. You will have to stay off it for a while."

The doctor wrapped her ankle with a bandage.

Then he got out a pair of crutches and showed Molly how to walk on them.

In the waiting room all the Scouts gathered around Molly.

"Wow!" said Roger. "Real crutches!"

"My brother had crutches once," said Mary Beth.

Rachel was standing in back by the door.

No one was fussing over her shiny skates now.

No one was noticing her blue pom-poms.

Rachel had never sprained her ankle.

She had never had crutches.

"Does it hurt?" asked Sonny.

"Put ice on it," said his mother.

"We must get Molly home and into a warm bed," said Mrs. Peters.

Everyone followed Molly out.
She led the parade, on her crutches.

# CHAPTER 8

# A Badge for Molly

Molly went to bed.

She had to miss school.

Everyone sent her cards.

The Pee Wee Scouts made their own cards.

Roger's had a girl skating on it.

It did not look like Molly. But Molly liked it.

Mary Beth drew a hospital bed on hers.

And she brought Molly candy. Chocolate-covered cherries!

Her favorites.

Mrs. Peters sent flowers, from the whole Pee Wee Scout Troop.

They made Molly's room look bright and cheery.

Every day after school some of the Scouts came to her house.

They played Candy Land.

Mary Beth brought Molly her homework and her school papers.

They wrote spelling words together.

"I wish I had a sprained ankle," said Rachel when she came to visit.

"You skate too well," said Molly. "You wouldn't fall on the ice."

"I used to fall when I was little," admitted Rachel. "It took me a long time to learn."

Molly wished she hadn't hexed Rachel.

And the good skaters.
It took time to learn to skate.
She could learn to skate too.
Once she got the right size skates.

The next week Molly went back to school.
She went on her crutches.
On Tuesday she went to Pee Wee Scouts on her crutches.
"I have some badges to give out," said Mrs. Peters. "Some of you get a skating badge."
Everyone clapped when the good skaters got their badges.
They all pinned them on their Scout kerchiefs or their shirts.
Next to their cookie badges.
The skating badge showed a picture of a skate.

A skate with no pom-poms.

Just a plain skate.

"I'll get that badge someday," said Molly.

"Of course," said Mrs. Peters.

"And now I have another badge. It is a badge for being a good patient."

Everyone knew who that badge was for!

The Pee Wee Scouts all looked at Molly.

"Molly Duff," said Mrs. Peters. "Come up and get your badge please."

Molly got up.

She walked to the front of the room on her crutches.

"Thank you," she said as she pinned it onto her blouse.

The badge was beautiful.
It had a little bed on it.
It looked like Molly's bed!

Across the bed was a little thermometer.

Around the edge it said THE GOOD PATIENT BADGE.

Molly hobbled back to her chair.

Everyone clapped.

She was glad to have a badge to pin on next to her cookie badge.

It wasn't as good as a skating badge.

But almost!

# Camp
# Ghost-Away

## JUDY DELTON

*Illustrated by Alan Tiegreen*

A YEARLING BOOK

For Jamie, Bandy, James, and Jim,
No matter who, I worship him.

# Contents

# CHAPTER 1

# A Mountain of Donuts

At last it was Tuesday. Tuesday was Pee Wee Scout Day. It took forever for Tuesday to come, thought Molly Duff.

Soon Troop 23 stood around the Scout table at Mrs. Peters's house. On the table were boxes and boxes of Scout donuts.

They were piled up like a mountain. A mountain of donuts. They had powdered sugar on them, like snow. Snow on the mountain, thought Molly.

Molly rubbed her stomach. She wished the Scouts could eat them. Eat the whole mountain.

"Now pay attention!" called Mrs. Peters. Mrs. Peters was their troop leader.

"Today we begin to sell our donuts. You'll go door to door on your own block. We must be very polite to people," said Mrs. Peters. "Even if they don't want to buy our donuts."

But they all will, thought Molly.

"We must count the money and give them the right change. And you have to be careful not to lose the money." Mrs. Peters explained everything to the Scouts so that they would know what to do. They all listened carefully. They were eager to get started.

"How much do they cost?" asked Sonny Betz.

"The donuts are one dollar a box," said Mrs. Peters. "Tell the people the money is for our trip to camp. If we sell enough donuts, our whole troop will go to Pee Wee Scout camp!"

All the Scouts cheered, "Yeah!"

"And the one who sells the most donuts will get an award," said Mrs. Peters. "It will be a special Scout badge. Are there any questions?"

Molly crossed her fingers. She didn't like questions. Questions took forever.

Rachel's hand went up. She always asked questions. Mrs. Peters called on Rachel. "Mrs. Peters, my mom says we should sell something that is more healthy.

Donuts have sugar. Sugar isn't good for your teeth."

A hex on Rachel's mother. Rachel's father was a dentist. Molly loved donuts.

"Donuts are all right if you don't eat too many, Rachel," said Mrs. Peters.

Before Rachel could say anything else and before any more questions, Mrs. Peters said, "Let's get out there and sell donuts! Let's sell enough to go to Pee Wee Scout camp!"

Troop 23 dashed for the door. Each Scout held a mountain of donuts. "I am going to sell the most!" said Molly.

"I am," said Lisa Ronning. "I am going to ask my grandma to buy some."

Molly wished that her grandma lived nearby. It was too far to go to sell donuts to her grandma. She would have to sell donuts to her own block.

"I'm going to sell a million donuts," said Rachel. Rachel always had to do better than anyone else. Even if donuts were bad for your teeth.

"You can't sell a million," scoffed Roger White. "Nobody can sell a million."
"I can," said Rachel.

"I'm going to go around a lot of blocks," said Sonny Betz. "Not just my own."
"Is your mama going with you?" Rachel called out.

Everyone knew Sonny was a mama's boy. He couldn't even walk to school alone. Lots of kids called Sonny a sissy.

"So what if she is?" said Sonny.

"Mama's boy, mama's boy!" shouted Rachel.

"Stuck up, stuck up!" returned Sonny.

"Let's sell donuts together," said Mary Beth Kelly to Molly. "It would be more fun, and we could go to more houses."

"Okay," said Molly.

When they got near their own block, Molly said, "Let's start here."

Mary Beth looked at the old house. A window was broken, and the paint was peeling.

"Mrs. Olson lives there," said Mary Beth. "She's mean. She doesn't like kids in her yard."

They kept walking to the next house. "Mrs. Cox is mean too," said Mary Beth.

14

*　　*　　*

"I'm going to the door anyway," said Molly bravely. She marched up to the door and knocked. An old lady came to the door.

"Do you want to buy some Scout donuts" asked Molly, "so we can go to camp?"

"I don't like donuts," said Mrs. Cox, slamming the door. Molly wanted to put a hex on Mrs. Cox, but she remembered what Mrs. Peters had said. Be polite even if they say no.

They went to the next house. Mary Beth went to the door. "Do you want to buy some Pee Wee donuts?" she asked.

"I have no teeth," said the old man who came to the door.

"You don't need teeth to eat these," said Mary Beth politely.

15

But he closed the door and did not answer.

The next person was not home. And the next man told them that he makes his own donuts.

"This is not as easy as I thought," said Molly. "We may never get to camp." She sighed.

Mary Beth sighed too.

They went to the last house on the block. A mother with three children came to the door. "Why, I'll take four boxes!" she said. "Two from each of you. We love donuts for dessert."

She gave the girls four dollars. "Have fun at camp!" she called.

CHAPTER **2**

# The Pee Wee Spirit

**M**olly and Mary Beth sold donuts all week long. They sold ten boxes each, and then they went back to ask Mrs. Peters for more donuts. By the next Tuesday they had each sold twelve boxes.

At three o'clock Molly went to Mary Beth's house. Then they walked to the Scout meeting together.

Everyone was turning in their donut money. Lisa Ronning turned in five dollars. Tim Noon turned in one dollar. Roger

White had sold sixteen boxes! But Sonny Betz and Rachel Myers had sold over one hundred boxes each!

"Wow!" said Molly. "There aren't even one hundred people on a whole block."

"That is really the Pee Wee spirit," said Mrs. Peters. "I think we should all clap for Sonny and Rachel!"

Everyone clapped their hands together, and shouted and whistled. Roger blew into his brown lunch bag. Then he punched it and the bag exploded. Pow!

Molly did not clap. She did not feel like cheering. She wanted to win.

"Maybe Rachel and Sonny will tell us how they sold so many donuts," said Mrs. Peters.

"My mom sold about eighty boxes at work," said Sonny proudly.

"Your mom!" shouted Roger. "That isn't

fair. You're supposed to sell them yourself!"

Leave it to Sonny, thought Molly, to
let his mom do it. Big baby!

"What's the matter with my mom selling them?" asked Sonny. Mrs. Peters said
it was all right to have your mother sell
your donuts.

"It doesn't matter who sells them," said
Mrs. Peters. "The more boxes that are
sold, the more money for Scout camp."

"Baby Sonny," muttered Roger.


"Now, Rachel, how did you sell so
many donuts?" asked Mrs. Peters.

"I sold them to my relatives," said Rachel, with her chin in the air. "We went
to a wedding, and my aunt and my
grandma bought twenty boxes each."

All of Rachel's family must be rich,
thought Molly.

"What will they do with all those donuts?" asked Mary Beth.

"They'll get fat!" shouted Molly, filling her cheeks with air. "They'll turn into donuts if they eat twenty boxes!"

Molly waddled across the floor, pretending to be Rachel's fat relatives.

Rachel looked very angry. Her face got red. "My grandma and my aunt are not fat!" she cried.

"They will be when they finish all those donuts," said Roger, holding his sides and chuckling.

"They aren't eating the donuts themselves," said Rachel. "They will give them to hungry people."

"The main thing is that we have enough money for camp," said Mrs. Peters. "And Rachel and Sonny get the award and the best donut seller's badge."

After Scouts, Molly said to Rachel, "You didn't sell a million boxes anyway. You said you were going to sell a million."

"Well, I sold a lot more than you," said Rachel. "Your dumb twelve boxes."

Molly couldn't argue with that. She wished a hex on Rachel's aunt and grandma. And on Sonny's mom. But she was glad that the Pee Wee Scouts (and their relatives) had earned enough for them to go to camp.

21

# Are We Almost There?

The next Tuesday, Troop 23 met again. Mrs. Peters talked about Camp Hide-Away. She told them what to bring. She told them what to wear. And she sent notes home to their mothers with the address and telephone number of the camp.

"We will leave Friday afternoon from the school," Mrs. Peters said. "We will ride to camp in a bus. We will come home on Sunday evening."

\*　　\*　　\*

Lisa's mother was coming along to help Mrs. Peters.

During the rest of the meeting the Scouts told good deeds they had done.

"I watered Mrs. Johnson's plants for her," said Tracy Barnes. "She's my next-door neighbor."

"I washed my dad's car," boasted Roger. "All by myself."

"Good for you!" said Mrs. Peters.

It was a short meeting. The Scouts sang their Pee Wee Scout song. Then they said the Pee Wee Scout pledge. Then they ran home to tell their parents about Camp Hide-Away.

"I've got a new swimsuit to take to camp," said Mary Beth at the park the next day. Some of the Pee Wees played there in the summer.

"I have a new swimsuit for camp too,"

called Molly from the top of the jungle gym.

"I've got two swimsuits," said Rachel. "My mom says everyone should have two. In case one is wet and you want to go in the water again."

Molly hung upside down by her knees. She tried to think of a worse word than hex. Molly learned "hex" from her grandma, but it wasn't really bad. She wanted a really bad word to use on Rachel's mother. Her mother was probably a show-off just like Rachel.

"I'm wearing my new bracelet to camp too," said Rachel. She held out her arm. "It is fourteen karat gold."

Rachel's bracelet sparkled in the sun. It looked very expensive. "My dad brought it back from New York with him," said Rachel.

*  *  *

Molly had a bracelet. But it was too small. And it was not real gold. It made her wrist turn green.

Rachel kept waving her arm so the bracelet would sparkle in Molly's eyes. Molly watched her. She wished the bracelet were hers.

The Pee Wees played in the park until suppertime. The next day they went there again. They had to wait and wait until Friday.

They ran under the sprinkler at Molly's house to make the time go faster.

They rode their skateboards in Roger's driveway to make the time go faster.

And they made lemonade at Lisa's, and tried to sell it on her front lawn, to make the time go faster. They sold only two cups. One to Lisa's mother. And one to her little brother. But he couldn't pay because he had lost his penny.

At last Friday came. All the Pee Wee Scouts carried their camp bags to the school. The school was closed, but the bus was waiting! Mrs. Peters and Mrs. Ronning were waiting too. Everyone got on the bus. Even Mrs. Peters's big black dog.

"He is coming along as our mascot," said Mrs. Peters. "His name is Tiny. He will be a watchdog in camp at night."

"Tiny!" shouted Tim. "His name should be Giant. Why would such a big dog be called Tiny?"

"Sometimes you call things the opposite of what they really are," explained Mrs. Peters. "Like sometimes if a man has no hair, they call him Curly."

The Scouts looked puzzled.

27

Then Roger said, "My uncle is real tall and everybody calls him Shorty!"

"That's right," said Mrs. Peters. "The opposite of what he is."

As the bus rolled along, the Scouts sang camp songs. They sang the Pee Wee Scout song too.

Mary Beth showed Molly her new swimsuit. And her new birthstone ring she got for her birthday. "Emerald," she said. "For May."

Rachel dangled her bracelet in front of everyone's eyes. Mary Beth's ring was almost as shiny.

"I don't feel so good," said Sonny. His face looked white. He leaned back in his seat and closed his eyes. He was sitting next to Lisa.

"OOOOOOoooo," he moaned, holding his stomach. "I think I'm carsick."

\* \* \*

28

Lisa leaned over into the aisle. She didn't want to sit too close to Sonny. He might have an accident. All over her.

Sonny groaned again, and the driver stopped the bus. He took Sonny off the bus until he felt better. But Sonny's face was still white when he got back on.

The Scouts looked out the windows.

They watched the trees and telephone poles whiz by.

"How much longer?" asked Mary Beth.
"Are we almost there?" asked Roger.

Just when the ride was getting boring and Roger and Sonny began to fight, Mrs. Peters said, "Here we are!"
Tiny began to bark. The bus squealed to a stop. The Pee Wees hurried to get off.

There were tall pine trees everywhere. There was a sparkly blue lake too. And right in the middle of the dark woods stood the tents.

"Do we have to sleep in a *tent*?" whined Rachel. "I thought there would be a hotel or something."

* * *

Roger laughed.

Sonny cracked up.

Even Mrs. Peters smiled. "This is a camp, Rachel. Camping is living outside, close to nature."

"Ugh, bugs," said Rachel, making a face.

"Bears!" said Roger. "Not just bugs!"

Rachel screamed. "Are there bears, Mrs. Peters?"

"There could be," she said. "But we are safe with Tiny. And we must not leave food outside."

Rachel looked as if she wanted to get back on the bus and go home.

"Scaredy cat," said Molly.

"Sissy," called the boys.

Four Scouts stayed in each tent. Mrs. Peters and Mrs. Ronning were not far

31

away. Tiny stayed in Molly's tent. And Mary Beth, Rachel, and Lisa. Each Scout had a cot and a sleeping bag.

After supper, Mrs. Peters and the Pee Wees built a campfire. Everyone held hands and sang around the campfire.

The fire made shadows in the woods. The moonlight shone on the lake. It was very pretty at camp. But it was scary, too, thought Molly.

The campfire burned low. Then it went out. Mrs. Peters led the Scouts in the Pee Wee Scout pledge. Everyone held hands while they said it. They always did that when they said the pledge.

Lisa's mother and Mrs. Peters helped the Scouts get tucked into the sleeping bags for the night. Then they went to their own tent.

"It's so quiet," said Lisa.

It was quiet. Except for the wind whistling around the tent, there wasn't a sound.

And it was dark. Pitch black, dark!

"I'm not scared, are you?" whispered Mary Beth.

"Naw," said Molly. But her voice sounded like it was shaking.

"We've got Tiny and Mrs. Peters and Lisa's mother to protect us," said Mary Beth with a quiver.

And then, just when they decided to be brave, they heard a loud ghostlike sound.

"OOOOOOOOOooooooooooooo," the ghost moaned. It sounded as if it were right outside their tent!

# CHAPTER 4
# Tiny Is a Hero

"What was that?" said Molly, leaping up from her cot. The other girls sat up. Mary Beth's eyes were wide open and as big as saucers. They all listened. They had goose bumps on their arms. But all they could hear now was the wind roaring in the trees.

"It was probably just an animal," said Lisa bravely. Lisa's mother was nearby. But not close enough, thought Lisa.

"What kind of animal makes a ghost noise?" asked Rachel.

"A wild animal," said Mary Beth, rolling her eyes toward the tent door.

"A wild animal!" yelled Rachel. "I want to go home! A wild animal could eat us! A wild animal is more dangerous than a ghost!"

Molly didn't know which was more dangerous. She didn't know if she would rather meet a ghost or a tiger. A ghost, she decided. No, a tiger, she thought, changing her mind.

"It's gone anyway," said Lisa, who felt she had to be brave. With her mother there, she couldn't be a sissy.

The children lay back on their cots. Just as they did, they heard the ghost-sound again. "OOOOOOOOOoooooooo." The voice carried on the wind. "OOOOOO-OOOooooooooeeeeeeee," it sounded again.

Molly screamed.

Mary Beth pulled her sleeping bag over her head.

Rachel cried.

Lisa got out of bed and crept to the door. She stuck her head out of the tent opening. But she held on to the sides so they did not flap in the wind. "I can't see anything in the dark," said Lisa.

Molly crept to the door beside Lisa.

The creature's loud voice rang out again, "*OOOOOO ooooo eeeee!*"

This time Tiny woke up and began to bark. The louder the creature's voice got, the louder Tiny barked. After a while he stopped barking. He threw back his head and howled. "Owwwooo!"

Molly was getting mad. She put her head out of the tent door and yelled, "A hex on you! Dumb ghost! Get out of our camp!"

The voice stopped. Tiny stopped howl-
ing.

Then the Scouts heard the voice say,
"I'm going to get yooooooou."

"That's no wild animal," said Molly.
"Animals can't talk."

"But ghosts can," said Lisa.

Now all four Pee Wees were at the
door of the tent. As they watched they
saw two white figures move in and out
of the trees.

"Look!" screamed Rachel. "There are
two ghosts!"

"HELLLLLP!" shouted all four girls.

The white shapes billowed in the wind.
Their floppy arms waved and they looked
as if they were floating!

All of a sudden Tiny dashed through
the door and began to chase the ghosts.
The girls chased Tiny.

Then the flaps on the other tents burst open and all the Scouts raced out!

They ran through the woods. The ghosts jumped over a creek with Tiny right behind.

Then the ghosts ran toward the camp. It seemed as if they couldn't see where they were going. Soon they bumped smack into the tent that was the kitchen.

Crash went the pots and pans!

Bang! The table toppled over.

Smash! The food fell from the cupboards.

It sounded like glass breaking. Wet things were dripping. By now everyone in the whole camp was awake and chasing the ghosts.

Suddenly a lantern came on, and light filled the kitchen tent.

"Yuck!" said Rachel. "I stepped in maple syrup."

The other Scouts were stepping in food
too. Food was all over. Chairs were on
their sides. The place was a mess.

40

*　　*　　*

The ghosts were under it all. They were trapped on the floor. Tiny had a foot on one ghost's body. He barked and barked.

"Tiny caught the ghosts!" cried Molly. "Tiny is a hero."

# CHAPTER 5
# Rat's Knees!

All of a sudden, one ghost started to cry. Mrs. Peters lifted the chairs and cleaned the food off his body. Then she shone the lantern over him.

"My legs are broken!" wailed the ghost. "And that dog walked on my stomach!"

The Scouts stared.

A ghost did not get broken legs, thought Molly. And do they have stomachs? Hey, that voice sounded familiar!

42

The ghost slowly got to his feet. The other ghost was still moaning.

"He has a sheet on!" said Mrs. Peters.

A real ghost did not wear a sheet, thought Molly. A real ghost was made out of something like smoke. White smoke. Something that was like a cloud. This was no cloud!

Mrs. Ronning marched up and pulled the sheet off of the ghost.

"Sonny Betz!" shouted the Pee Wee Scouts. "It's not a ghost, it's Sonny Betz!"

"Roger made me do it!" he shouted. He pointed to the other ghost.

Some of the Scouts began to laugh. Some of them called him names. "Dumb bunny Sonny!"

Molly did not laugh. Being scared in the woods at night was not funny.

43

44

A hex on Sonny Betz.

A hex on Roger White.

A double hex.

Sonny was still sobbing in pain. Mrs. Ronning checked his legs. She felt all his bones. He cried louder. "Nothing is broken," said Mrs. Ronning.

"He made me do it," said Sonny again, pointing.

Mrs. Peters pulled the sheet off the other ghost. Sure enough, it was Roger.

"It was his idea!" Sonny cried. "Roger said we should scare the girls."

Roger did not look hurt. He looked sheepish. He looked as if he would like to dash out the door and run away. "It was just a joke," muttered Roger.

\*      \*      \*

45

Molly felt like giving Roger and Sonny a big smack. Pow! Bang!

But Mrs. Peters said, "I think the ghosts have suffered enough. I hope they learned a lesson. Jokes are dangerous. They could have been hurt."

"This camp is named wrong," said Mary Beth. "Instead of Camp Hide-Away, I think we should call it Camp Ghost-Away!"

"Yeah!" shouted Molly. "That is a good name."

In the morning Mrs. Peters made Roger and Sonny clean up the mess in the kitchen.

Everyone was yawning when they came to breakfast. They had all missed a lot of sleep because of the ghosts. But when the food came, they were hungry.

"Pancakes." said Mary Beth. "I love pancakes."

Rachel said, "I don't eat pancakes. My dad says there's too much sugar in them."

Molly groaned. Rachel was a fussbudget. She just drank orange juice and ate some grapefruit.

Molly made a face at the grapefruit. "Sour," she said. "It gives me the creeps. Yuck!"

"You'll be sorry when all your teeth fall out," said Rachel.

"Teeth-schmeeth," said Molly. "My teeth are as good as yours."

Later that morning, Mrs. Peters said, "Everyone into your swimsuits."

When the Pee Wees were ready, she said, "Let's see if you can learn to float. When you can float alone, you will get the Pee Wee float badge."

"You can't float," said Rachel to Molly. "You ate too many pancakes."

Molly wanted to stick out her tongue. She wanted to hex her. She wanted to say a bad word.

All of a sudden she shouted out, "Rat's knees!"

It felt good. It was better than a hex. Rats were ugly things. It was a bad word. And a new one!

When they got to the beach there was a lifeguard. He looked old, maybe eighteen. His name was Rick. He showed them how to do the dead man's float.

"Just relax," said Rick. "Then your body will float."

The Pee Wees tried it. Rick held his arms under each of them at first. Then he let go.

When he let go of Lisa, she floated!

When he let go of Tim, he floated!

But when he let go of Molly, she began to sink. Plunk, plunk, plunk.

Molly's feet sank down. Right down to the bottom of the lake. She could touch even the ground with her toes!

Molly kicked her legs to get them up. She got a big gulp of lake water.

"I can't do it," she sputtered. Then some water went up her nose.

"I told you, you ate too many pancakes!" Rachel said. Rachel could float before she came to camp. She had had private swimming lessons in kindergarten.

Rat's knees! A hex on Rachel.

"Don't worry," said Rick the lifeguard. "It takes time to learn to float. You have to relax all of your muscles."

Molly felt like crying. She even felt

49

like going home. It was no fun to be a failure. She was as smart as they were. Why couldn't she float? Maybe Rachel was right! She was too fat!

Rachel went to the tent and changed into her other swimsuit.

Molly practiced floating with Rick. But she still sank. Soon it was time to go out in the rowboat. Molly still could not float.

Rick showed them how to row. Sonny tried it. His oars flopped around, but the small rowboat moved.

"Good!" said Rick.

50

Then Roger rowed. He got water in the
boat. The girls got wet.

"Hey, stop it!" said Rachel. "I just got
all dried off!"

But Rick said, "Good!"

Then it was Molly's turn.

Molly pulled on one oar. Then the other. The oars were heavy. She felt one begin to slip. Ker-plop! One of the oars fell off the boat. It sank to the bottom of the lake as the Pee Wees watched.

Rick did not say Good. He said, "How are we going to get in to shore?" He had to row all the way in with one oar. It took a long time.

"Ho-ho! What a rower!" shouted Roger. He made sounds like the oar going into the water. "Ker-plop, ker-plop." Everyone laughed.

Molly was getting tired of camp. Everyone could learn camp things but her.

After lunch, the Pee Wee Scouts went on a nature hike with Mrs. Peters. They looked for seeds and berries. They listened to the birds sing. Mary Beth found a stone that was an agate. Rachel found a robin's blue eggshell. Tim Noon found a rare wildflower. But Molly got poison ivy.

"Now, everyone, look here," said Mrs. Peters. "Stay away from this plant. It has three leaves together. It looks just like the picture in our nature book."

The Scouts all looked at it closely. "That was dumb," said Rachel. "Why did you touch it?"

"It doesn't look like the picture in the book," muttered Molly. She scratched and scratched.

Mrs. Peters put some lotion on her arms. She still itched. Rat's knees!

# CHAPTER 6
# I Want My Mother

Everyone was tired by suppertime. Everyone but Rachel. She put on a new outfit for supper. It had an anchor on the shirt and a whistle around the neck.

Rachel made a face. "I hate hot dogs!" she said. "I thought we'd have a picnic with steak and stuff."

After supper the Scouts had a treasure hunt. Then they sang around the campfire. They sang the Pee Wee Scout song.

Rachel got ashes and mustard on her new outfit. And Roger pushed her into the lake with her new sandals on.

Camp wasn't so bad after all, thought Molly. Even though her arms were still itching.

Soon it was dark. Everyone helped put the campfire out. All of a sudden there was the sound of someone crying. Molly looked around. Sonny was sitting on a tree stump. Tears were running down his face.

Mrs. Peters went over to him and said, "What's the matter, Sonny? What happened?"

Sonny cried even louder. He buried his face in his hands. Everyone ran over to see why he was crying.

"I want my mother!" screamed Sonny. "I want to go home!"

55

Mrs. Peters put her arm around Sonny.
"You're just homesick," she said. "You
will feel better in the morning."

"Baby," muttered Rachel. "Mama's boy."

Mrs. Peters tried to make Sonny feel better. She gave him warm milk and tucked him into his sleeping bag. Sonny still sobbed.

"He is really spoiled," said Rachel when they were in bed. "Can't even leave his mother when he's in first grade. Yuck!"

In the middle of the night Sonny came to the girls' tent. He was carrying a blanket and crying. He was not playing ghost now.

"I want to go home!" he screamed.

Mrs. Peters heard the noise and came running.

"I want to go home," wailed Sonny. "Right now!"

57

All of the Pee Wee Scouts were up now. They wondered what Mrs. Peters would do.

"You should have stayed home," muttered Roger. "Babies shouldn't come to camp."

Sonny wailed louder. "I feel sick," he said, holding his stomach.

"Homesick," said Mrs. Peters. "You are just homesick, Sonny."

"It feels awful," sobbed Sonny.

"I guess the only thing to do is to call Sonny's mother," said Mrs. Peters.

Sonny threw his arms around Mrs. Peters. "Call her!" he cried. "Tell her to come and get me right away!"

Mrs. Peters went up the hill to the campground office to use the telephone. When she came back Sonny was still sobbing.

"Is she coming? Is she coming?" he asked.

"Yes," said Mrs. Peters. "She is leaving right away."

No one could sleep because of all the excitement. "Sonny's mama has to rescue him!" sang Roger.

"Mama's boy, mama's boy," sang Rachel.

"Rat's knees!" said Molly.

* * *

At last Sonny's mother came. Sonny leaped into the car and hugged her. "Take me home!" he cried.

Mrs. Betz put her arms around Sonny and hugged him.

The Scouts giggled. Mrs. Betz drank a cup of coffee and then they left.

Finally the camp was settled down for the night.

Molly was almost asleep, when she heard a sound. What was it? She listened closely. Someone else was crying. It was Rachel!

Molly crept over to her cot. "What is the matter with you?"

"I'm homesick too." She sniffed. "I want my mother!"

Suddenly Molly heard something else. It was Mary Beth! She was crying into

60

her pillow too. And so was Lisa! Even though her mother was close by.

"Rat's knees!" said Molly. "I'm the only one here who isn't homesick!"

# CHAPTER 7

# Molly the Brave

The Pee Wee Scouts slept late. When they got up for breakfast they found out that lots of them had been homesick. Tim and Roger had been crying. And two girls in the tent next to Molly's had cried too.

"I guess Molly is the brave one." said Mrs. Peters. "The only one who didn't get homesick!"

"It's not my fault," grumbled Rachel. "My mom said Pee Wee Scouts are pretty young to be gone overnight."

"Homesickness is an awful thing," said Mrs. Peters. "It feels like real sickness. It is nothing to be ashamed of."

"See?" said Rachel to Molly, making a face. Molly made a face back. Molly was still the bravest! She was still the only one who was not homesick. That meant she acted older than six. It meant she was more grown up than the other Pee Wee Scouts.

Molly the brave. Rat's knees! That sounded good.

Rick came to get the Scouts for swimming. Molly still could not float. But when they went rowing, she did not drop the oar in the water. She rowed a little way by herself. But the boat kept turning around in a circle. Rick helped her. He showed her which oar to pull.

*  *  *

After lunch the Scouts took naps. Then Mrs. Peters showed them how to weave baskets out of straw. They took their baskets down the road to pick some wild berries. Mrs. Ronning went too.

Rachel had another new camp outfit on. It was bright pink.

Rat's knees! thought Molly. Rachel must be rich. Rachel's gold bracelet sparkled in the sun. Mary Beth's ring sparkled too.

"Is this a berry?" called Roger, holding up something red.

"No, Roger, that isn't a berry we can eat. Be careful to pick only the kind I showed you," said Mrs. Peters.

"What about this?" said Rachel, waving something blue in her hand.

"That is a grape," said Mrs. Peters. "That is all right to pick."

"Don't you know what a *grape* is, dummy?" said Roger.

Rachel made a face. She didn't like to crawl on the ground to get berries. Berries stained. Her new outfit would get dirty. And her hair got all messed up on the twigs and low branches.

Molly had a lot of berries in her basket. She found a patch of red, red strawberries. And a patch of blue, blue blueberries. She would have more berries than anyone!

"I hate these bugs!" shouted Rachel. "They're flying in my eyes!" She waved her arms at the bugs.

"Put some of this on, Rachel," called Mrs. Peters. She handed her a can of bug spray.

"Yuck!" said Rachel. "That makes me smell! It makes my hair ishy! My mom doesn't like me to use that."

"You'll be scratching tonight," said Mrs. Peters. "Mosquitoes bite."

Rat's knees! Rachel should have stayed home, thought Molly. She didn't like the camp food. She didn't like bug spray. She didn't like tents. She was homesick. Rachel Myers was a big baby.

Soon most of the troop's baskets were filled. "Let's start back to camp now," said Mrs. Peters, counting noses.

The Pee Wee Scouts followed Mrs. Peters. They were all scratching. They had berry juice on their arms. They were sunburned too.

When they got back to camp, Mary Beth said, "My ring is lost!"

She held up her hand. Sure enough, the little gold ring was not on her finger.

She had it on when they left to pick berries. Molly had seen it.

"Oh, dear!" said Mrs. Peters. She frowned.

"I'll bet someone stole it," said Rachel.

"No one took it," said Mrs. Peters. "It must have fallen off when we were picking berries."

Mary Beth looked as if she wanted to cry. "It was real gold," she said. "My aunt gave it to me."

"It is best to leave jewelry at home when we camp," said Mrs. Peters. She looked at Rachel's gold bracelet. Rachel put her arm behind her back.

"Don't worry, Mary Beth," said Mrs. Peters. "We will find your ring." Everyone set their baskets down on a camp table and went back to look for Mary Beth's ring. Even Rachel.

\*　　\*　　\*

"Rat's knees!" said Molly. "It could be
buried in all this grass."

The Scouts looked everywhere Mary

Beth had been. They looked under leaves. They looked on low branches. They looked in the ditches beside the road. No ring.

Then it began to get dark. They would have to leave it. The Pee Wees were going home tonight.

"Someone will have to drive out and look tomorrow, when it is light," said Mrs. Peters.

Mary Beth was very brave. She looked as if she might cry, but she didn't. She began to sort the berries with the other Scouts.

Suddenly Molly had an idea. She went over to the basket that Mary Beth had used. Molly shook the basket. Sure enough, it made a noise. A noise that berries did not make. Clink, clink, clink!

Molly tipped the basket and reached her hand down to the bottom. There was something hard there. Something hard and round and shiny. It was a ring!

"Look!" shouted Molly, running over to Mary Beth. "I found it!"

Now Mary Beth was crying. But they were tears of happiness. She threw her arms around Molly and hugged her.

"It must have slipped off my finger when I put berries in the basket," she said. "It is a little bit too big for me."

All the Scouts clapped for Molly. Rat's knees! This was the second fun thing that happened to her at camp! And now it was time to leave. Just when things were getting good.

# 8
# Badges

The Pee Wee Scouts fell asleep on the way back to town. They were too tired to sing. They were too tired to talk. Camp had worn them out.

"The park will be boring now," said Lisa.

"But we have Scouts on Tuesday," said Mary Beth. "The day after tomorrow."

Everyone was eager for Tuesday to come. On Tuesday they would get their badges. The donut badges. The swimming badges. The rowing badges. The nature badges. All the camp badges!

But Molly had no badge to wait for. She had not sold one hundred donuts. She could not float. She could not row. She did not find a rock or a wildflower.

When Tuesday came around, the Pee Wees met at Mrs. Peters's house. It will be boring to watch the others get badges, thought Molly. She sat on the floor and

pretended to be snoring. Boring, boring, boring. Snoring boring.

"Now!" said Mrs. Peters loudly. "What did you like best about camp?"

"Swimming!" said Rachel.

"Rowing!" said Lisa.

"Being a ghost!" said Roger.

"Finding my ring," said Mary Beth.

Molly wished Mrs. Peters would give out the badges. She wanted to get it over with. Finally Mrs. Peters held up a pile of badges. All the Scouts cheered. Except Molly.

"The first badge," said Mrs. Peters, "is for selling the most donuts. We all know who gets that badge! Rachel and Sonny are tied for first place, and Roger comes in second."

Rachel and Sonny went up to get their badges. Then Roger went up. Everyone clapped. A hex on them, thought Molly. And a hex on donuts.

Sonny's mother clapped loudly. She was the only mother at the meeting. Baby Sonny. Homesick Sonny. Rat's knees!

Mrs. Peters called Tim Noon for the nature badge. She called Rachel and Mary Beth for the swimming badge. And Roger got a badge for rowing.

Soon almost everyone had a badge. Or two or three. Molly was not bored anymore. She was hurt. She felt left out. She was the only one who did not get any badge at all.

Molly felt a tear start to roll down her cheek. Oh, no, she thought, I don't want to cry.

"Molly Duff!" called Mrs. Peters.

Molly sat up.

"Come up," said Mrs. Peters. "I have a badge for you."

Molly wondered what badge she could

get. She had not earned any. But she got up and walked to the front of the room.

"This is a new badge," Mrs. Peters said. "Just for Molly. I made it up specially for her. It's the 'I didn't get homesick' badge!"

Mrs. Peters pinned the badge on Molly's blouse. Everyone clapped. Molly grinned. She wasn't bored now. Or hurt.

"And I have one more," said Mrs. Peters. "This is specially for Molly too. She is the only one at camp who earned this badge. And it is an important one."

She pinned another badge on Molly's blouse. It was a "finder's badge."

"Finding Mary Beth's ring deserves a badge," said Mrs. Peters.

The Pee Wee Scouts clapped again. Molly had been last, but she wasn't least.

It was true she could not float. And
she could not row very well. But she did
find the ring. And she was the only one
at camp who was not homesick!

Rat's knees! she thought. Why can't
Pee Wee camp last all summer!

♪ ♫ Pee Wee Scout Song ♪ ♫
(to the tune of
"Old MacDonald Had a Farm")

Scouts are helpers, Scouts have fun,
Pee Wee, Pee Wee Scouts!
We sing and play when work is done,
Pee Wee, Pee Wee Scouts!

With a good deed here,
And an errand there,
Here a hand, there a hand,
Everywhere a good hand.

Scouts are helpers, Scouts have fun,
Pee Wee, Pee Wee Scouts!

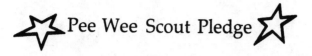 Pee Wee Scout Pledge

We love our country
And our home,
Our school and neighbors too.

As Pee Wee Scouts
We pledge our best
In everything we do.

# Lucky
# Dog Days
## JUDY DELTON

*Illustrated by Alan Tiegreen*

A YOUNG YEARLING BOOK

For Julie:
Though you are far across the sea
You're still the whole wide world to me.

# Contents

# CHAPTER 1

# Not Christmas

The Pee Wee Scouts scrambled out of cars. They ran into Mrs. Peters's house.

It was Tuesday. Time for a Pee Wee Scout meeting.

Mrs. Peters was smiling. She was their troop leader.

When everyone sat down, she said, "This is a special month. Does anyone know why it is special?"

"Christmas?" said Roger White.

All the Scouts laughed.

1

Roger's face turned red.

"Christmas is in winter," said Molly Duff.

"It's hot outside now and there are flowers," said Rachel Myers. She laughed at Roger.

"Some places have flowers at Christmas," said Mrs. Peters. "Like California and Hawaii."

"Ha," said Roger. He stuck his tongue out at Rachel.

Rachel raised her hand to tell Mrs. Peters.

"Tattletale," said Roger.

Mrs. Peters frowned. "The special thing about this month is not Christmas," she said.

"Is it March of Dimes month?" asked Rachel. "My dad says that's a good cause."

"No, but you're getting closer," said Mrs. Peters.

"I know!" said Sonny Betz. "I'll bet it is National Secretaries' month." Sonny's mother was a secretary.

Mrs. Peters shook her head.

"Is it Eat More Pork month?" asked Mary Beth Kelly. She remembered seeing some pigs on TV. And pork chops and sausages.

"Oink, oink," said Molly.

The rest of the Scouts began to snort.

"Well, I'll tell you," said Mrs. Peters. "It is Help-a-Pet month."

"I've got a pet!" called out Tracy Barnes. "I've got a gerbil."

Tracy's nose was running.

It was always running, thought Molly.

"That's a dumb pet," said Roger. "A dog is the best kind of pet."

Tracy looked like she was going to cry. "Snuffy isn't dumb," she said. "He can roll over and play dead."

3

"A gerbil?" said Molly. "A gerbil can't play dead!"

The Scouts who had cats for pets were chasing Roger around the room. "Dogs are not the best!" they shouted. "Cats are."

"I've got a horse," said Rachel.
Rat's knees! thought Molly. Rachel *would* have to have something bigger than anyone else.
Mrs. Peters held up her hand.
The Pee Wees knew that meant quiet.
"Dogs are good for some people," she said. "And cats and horses are good for others. And gerbils are good pets too."
She smiled at Tracy.
"My mom says house pets are dirty," said Rachel. She tossed her head. "Cats lick butter and shed on your clothes."

4

"My cat doesn't lick the butter," said Lisa Ronning.

"As I said," Mrs. Peters went on, "this

5

is Help-a-Pet month. I wondered how many of you would like to help a pet?"

All the Pee Wees raised their hands.

"What pets?" asked Roger. "My dog doesn't need help."

Rachel snickered.

"I was thinking of homeless pets," said Mrs. Peters. "Pets who have no one to love them. There are lots of pets at the animal shelter that have no homes. Maybe Troop 23 could take them for walks. Or raise money for more kennels. They are very short of space."

"Maybe we can adopt them," said Sonny Betz.

"Ho, ho," said Mary Beth. "How can we adopt a hundred dogs?"

The Scouts broke out into laughter again.

Mrs. Peters's dog Tiny ran into the room. He barked and barked.

6

"He likes the idea of adopting all the
dogs," said Mrs. Peters. She laughed. "But
we can't adopt them. We can only help
them."

The Scouts cheered. It would be fun to help a pet.

For the rest of the meeting they all played Scout games.

Then they had milk and chocolate chip cookies.

They reported some good deeds they had done for others during the week.

Then everyone stood up to say the Pee Wee Scout pledge. And sing the Pee Wee Scout song.

After that it was time to go.

On her way home, Molly thought, Next week we're going to help a pet!

# CHAPTER 2

# Trouble with Snooks

Next Tuesday took forever to come.

The Pee Wees rode their skateboards to make the time go faster.

It was a hot, hot August.

They went swimming at the pool.

They climbed trees in the park.

Still it took a long time for Tuesday to come.

Finally it was time for the Pee Wees to meet again. They were going to the animal shelter for their meeting.

As they tumbled out of the cars at the shelter they could hear barks. And meows. They heard whines and whimpering.

"Someone is crying," said Mary Beth.

A lady came out to meet them. "I will take you on a tour," she said.

The Scouts followed the lady. Her name was Miss Penn.

"This is our cat room," she said.

Cages, cages, cages.

All around the room were cages.

In every cage was a cat.

Striped cats. White cats. Brown cats. Cats with long hair. Cats with short hair. Big cats. Little cats. Medium cats.

Every cat was crying. They wanted the Scouts to take them out. They put their paws through the bars. "Me-ow," they called. Take me home.

Miss Penn opened a cage door. She

took out a tiger cat. She put him in Molly's arms.

"Oooh!" squealed Molly. "He is so soft. I wish I could take him home."

Miss Penn handed each Scout a cat to hold.

When she gave Tracy a cat, she began to sneeze. Then her eyes started to tear. Tracy's nose started to run too. More than usual, thought Molly. Yuck.

"You must be allergic," said Mrs. Peters.

She took the cat and put it back in the cage.

The longer they were in the shelter, the more Tracy sneezed.

When they got to the dog room, the dogs barked at them. Tracy's eyes were nearly swollen shut.

"Dear me," said Mrs. Peters to Tracy. "You will have to wait in the car."

11

12

"My cousin is allergic too," said Rachel. "He has to get shots."

"Sonny is allergic," said Roger. "That's why he couldn't come today."

"That's not why he stayed home," said Tim Noon. "He didn't come because he's scared of dogs!"

"Baby," said Rachel. "Only babies are afraid of dogs."

More dogs began to bark. Arf! Arf!

"Now!" said Mrs. Peters loudly. "Miss Penn said these dogs would love to have a walk. You may each choose a dog and take it for a short walk around the shelter yard."

Molly wanted the cocker spaniel.

So did Roger.

"There are plenty of dogs to go around," Mrs. Peters said.

"Selfish," said Molly to Roger as she chose a beagle in the next cage.

Mary Beth chose a poodle.

13

Tim chose a dog that looked like a spaniel in front and a Labrador in back.

"He is a Heinz dog," said Mrs. Peters. "Fifty-seven varieties!"

Lisa chose a terrier.

And Rachel chose a St. Bernard called Snooks.

"That is a pretty big dog," said Miss Penn.

"Do you think you can handle him?" asked Mrs. Peters.

Rachel nodded. "My uncle has a Great Dane," she said. "I always take him for a walk."

"Liar!" said Molly.

Rachel made a face at Molly.

When they got outside, Molly's beagle walked at her heels.

So did Mary Beth's poodle.

Lisa's terrier ran and tugged at his leash. Lisa pulled him toward her.

But when Snooks got to the door, he took off like a bullet. He ran toward a little pond and he pulled Rachel with him.

"Help!" shouted Rachel as she flew past the girls.

The other dogs saw Snooks and they began to run too.

They each pulled a Scout along behind them.

Tim's Heinz dog got so excited that he ran around Tim in circles. He wrapped the leash around Tim's legs.

"Hey," called Tim. "I'm all tied up!"

Soon all the dogs were racing toward the pond behind Snooks. They pulled the Pee Wees behind them, all except Tim. He was on the ground. He tried to get unwound.

The dogs ran amuck.

The Scouts were yelling and shouting.
"Let go of the leash!" called Roger.
Everyone did.
Everyone but Rachel.

16

# CHAPTER 3
# Soaked!

"Splash!" went Snooks into the pond.
"Splash!" went Rachel right after him.
Tim finally got his legs free.

Roger and Tim ran to the pond. They grabbed Rachel's arms and pulled her out. She was dripping wet and she had a water lily on top of her head.

Molly and Lisa and Mary Beth got there next. Then Mrs. Peters and Miss Penn.

"I thought you said you walked a Great Dane!" said Roger.

Miss Penn went back to the shelter and got a towel. She wrapped the towel around Rachel.

"My new shorts!" moaned Rachel. "They're ruined."

All of a sudden Molly began to laugh. Rachel looked so funny dripping wet.

With a water lily on her head.

And her clothes soaked.

Roger and Tim and Lisa and Mary Beth began to laugh too. The other Scouts joined in.

When Miss Penn and Mrs. Peters saw that Rachel was all right, they laughed too.

Roger ran off to catch Snooks.

Snooks thought he was playing. When Roger got close to him, Snooks ran. He looked like he was smiling. At last Roger caught him.

Arf! Arf! Snooks barked loudly.

The rest of the dogs had jumped into the pond and were swimming around. Then they came out, dripping wet.

Roger and Tim rounded up all the dogs.

"They needed the exercise," said Miss Penn, laughing.

"Well I didn't," said Rachel, pouting. "I don't want to help a pet anymore."

"Instead of Rachel walking a dog," said Lisa, "a dog walked Rachel!"

Rachel was still wrapped in the towel. She went to sit in the car with Tracy.
Soon everyone began to calm down.
They gave the dogs a short walk.
Molly tried to teach the beagle to sit up.
Tim played fetch with his mutt.

"I think we have had enough for one day," said Mrs. Peters. "It's time to leave."

When the Scouts got back to Mrs. Peters's house, they drew pictures of the pets they had helped.
Molly's beagle had a red collar.
Mary Beth's dog looked like he had a plate on his head. "That's his topknot!"

said Mary Beth. "Poodles have topknots and pom-poms."

"Ho, ho," Roger laughed. "It looks like a hat."

Roger held his picture up. It was a picture of a pond. In the pond was a girl with a lily on her head.

The girl was Rachel.

"It's not funny!" shouted Rachel. "You tear that up, Roger White, or I'll tell my mother."

She began to chase Roger.

Roger held the paper over his head.

Mrs. Peters had to clap her hands.

The room grew quiet.

"Scouts," she said. "I have thought of a way to earn money to help a pet. We will have a rummage sale. Ask your mothers and fathers if they have anything to donate. Ask your neighbors too."

\*    \*    \*

22

Troop 23 sang their Scout song.

Then they said the Pee Wee Scout pledge.

Time to go home, thought Molly.

She was tired.

Help-a-Pet month was hard work.

# CHAPTER 4
# Diamond Rummage

On Saturday morning, Tracy dialed Molly's phone number. "Let's go collect rummage today," she said.

Even over the phone Molly could tell that Tracy's nose was running.

"I'm going with Mary Beth," said Molly.

"I'll come too," said Tracy, hanging up.

"Rat's knees!" said Molly. She stamped her foot. She didn't want to go with Tracy.

Tracy was bossy. And she was always sniffling.

It made Molly sick to her stomach.

Molly and Mary Beth tried to sneak off without Tracy, but when they left they could see her down the street.

She was coming toward them.

She was pulling a big red wagon.

On the side of it, it said HELP A PET.

"We can put all the stuff in this," she called.

Molly and Mary Beth each had a big bag. They had not thought to bring a wagon.

"You can't get much in those bags," said Tracy. "Let's go down to Lake Street, where all the big houses are."

The girls followed Tracy.

Rat's knees! thought Molly. Tracy always gets her own way.

*   *   *

At the first house, the lady had no rummage to donate.

At the next house, no one was home.

But at the big white house on the corner, the lady said, "I like pets. I'll see what I can find."

The Scouts waited while the lady went into her closet.

She came out with five belts. And a sparkling necklace. Plus a bracelet with a blue stone in it.

"Thank you very much," said the Pee Wees.

"Do you think those are real diamonds?" asked Mary Beth, pointing to the necklace.

They watched the stones sparkle in the sun.

"We'll get a lot of money for the animal shelter if they are!" said Tracy. She wiped her nose with the back of her sleeve.

The girls collected more belts and jewelry. They collected some dresses and shoes. They even got some baby clothes at one house. One man gave them two winter coats.

People liked to help pets. The girls filled the whole wagon. The brown bags were filled up too. The bags were heavy.

"Set them in the wagon on top of the coats," said Tracy. "Then we can go to one more house."

"We've got enough," said Molly. "I'm hot. Let's go home."

Mary Beth wanted to go home too.

"Just one more house," said Tracy, sniffling. "This big one here with the rose garden."

The girls sighed. They followed Tracy up the walk to the door. On the door

was a sign that said:

DELIVERIES USE BACK DOOR.

"Is that us?" whispered Mary Beth.

"Not exactly," said Tracy.

28

But the girls trudged around to the back. They rang the doorbell again and again. Finally a man looked out the window. He looked mean.

"We are collecting rummage," shouted Tracy. "To help pets."

"I don't like pets," said the man. "Go away."

"What a crab," muttered Molly. "A hex on that guy."

"We don't care," said Mary Beth. "We've got piles of stuff. We'll have more than anybody else."

The girls walked past the rose garden.

They walked down the sidewalk to where they had left the red wagon.

Then they stopped.

"Rat's knees!" said Molly. "Our wagon is gone!"

# CHAPTER 5

# The Red Wagon

**J**ust then a big car drove by.

A girl was leaning out the window. "Hey!" she called out, and waved.

It was Rachel. Her mother was driving the car. It was filled with rummage for the sale.

"Have you seen a red wagon filled with rummage?" asked Tracy.

Rachel shook her head. Her mother drove off.

"I'll bet she took it," said Tracy.

"She didn't take it," said Mary Beth. "She has enough stuff of her own."

"It's your fault," grumbled Molly to Tracy. "You made us go to one more house."

The girls looked behind bushes and trees.

They looked to see if the wagon had rolled down the hill.

"It's gone," said Tracy. Her nose was really running now.

Yuck, thought Molly. But it was sad that Tracy had lost her wagon.

"Let's go tell Mrs. Peters what happened," said Mary Beth.

The girls walked slowly toward their leader's house.

They had no red wagon to pull.

They had no bags to carry.

They had no rummage to sell to help a pet.

When they got to Mrs. Peters's house, Rachel's car was in front. Rachel and her mother were carrying things into the garage for the sale.

"Hello!" called Mrs. Peters. "Did you come to help?"

Molly nodded. They could help sort the clothes. And put price tags on them.

"Why, just look at the carload of things that Rachel brought," Mrs. Peters said.

Molly looked.

A hex on Rachel. She always had to have the most of everything.

Even rummage.

"My goodness! Just look at the big load of things the boys are bringing," called Mrs. Peters from the doorway.

"What hardworking Pee Wees you boys are!" she said.

Molly turned around to look.

In the doorway stood Roger and Sonny and Tim.

Right beside them was Tracy's red wagon.

It was filled with coats and shoes and belts and jewelry!

# CHAPTER 6

# How Much Is That Doggy?

"Our diamonds!" shouted Tracy.

"Our belts and shoes and coats," said Mary Beth.

"You stole our rummage!" shouted Molly.

She wanted to go over and grab the diamonds out of Roger's hand.

She wanted to hit him. Smack, Smack, Smack!

She could too. She was strong.

But she didn't want to start a fistfight in Mrs. Peters's garage.

"This is our rummage," said Tim. "We found it sitting right on the sidewalk."

"It belongs to us!" shouted Tracy. "That's my wagon! And those are our diamonds."

"Prove it," said Roger. "I don't see your name on it."

All three girls talked at once. They told Mrs. Peters how they came out of the mean man's yard and found their wagon was gone.

"Nobody was near it," muttered Sonny. "How did we know it was yours?"

Tracy grabbed her red wagon back. She stuck her tongue out at the boys.

"The main thing is," said Mrs. Peters brightly, "that this rummage will help the homeless pets. No matter whose it is!"

But it *did* matter, thought Molly.

We worked hard to get that rummage! Harder than Rachel.

Much, much harder than Roger, Tim, and Sonny.

The girls grumbled as they unloaded the wagon.

"What price should we put on the diamonds?" asked Mary Beth.

"We won't put a price on them," said Mrs. Peters. "We will sell them to the highest bidder. That way your necklace will bring in a lot of money for the shelter. It may not be made of real diamonds, but it is very pretty."

On the day of the sale, everyone was there.

All the Pee Wees.

All the parents.

All the neighbors.

HELP A PET, said a banner stretched across the top of the garage.

Tiny welcomed all the buyers with loud barks.

A sign in front of Mrs. Peters's house said, PEE WEE SCOUT SALE HERE TODAY! HELP A PET.

"Is he for sale?" asked one lady, pointing to Tiny.

"Oh, no," said Mrs. Peters. "He's my dog."

Molly had an idea! She leaned over and whispered into Mrs. Peters's ear.

Mrs. Peters grinned. "I think that's a wonderful idea, Molly," she said.

Then Mrs. Peters and Molly got into her car.

"We'll be right back," they called.

They drove to the animal shelter.

*　　*　　*

When they returned, Miss Penn was in the car. So were six cages, with a dog in each one!

"Kevin," called Mrs. Peters. "Could you boys help us with these?"

Roger and Sonny grabbed one cage.

Kevin and Tim grabbed another.

They lined them up in front of the garage.

"It looks like this is the animal shelter!" yelled Roger.

"Or a pet shop," said Sonny.

The people who came to buy rummage had to walk past the cages first.

"A dog sale to help dogs!" said Tim.

"It was Molly's idea," said Mrs. Peters.

"A super idea," Miss Penn agreed.

"We can find some good homes for the dogs and earn money for the shelter at the same time," Roger said.

# CHAPTER 7

# A Thousand Dollars for the Dogs

**B**y noon, all the dogs were sold except one.

"They are going like hotcakes," said Miss Penn. "I'll go back and get some more. And I'll bring a cat or two."

"That was really smart," said Mary Beth to Molly. "How did you ever think of that?"

"When the lady wanted to buy Tiny," Molly explained. "She gave me the idea that we could sell dogs."

41

"Dogs make good rummage," said Mrs. Peters, smiling. "Molly is our Pee Wee hero today."

"I could have thought of that," said Rachel. "It's not so great."

"You're just jealous," said Tracy.

"Rachel's jealous, Rachel's jealous!" sang Sonny and Roger and Tim all together.

It was very crowded at the sale. All the rummage was selling quickly. There were just a few things left.

"Now," said Mrs. Peters. "I would like your attention please! It is time to bid for the necklace. Who can give us the largest bid to help the animal shelter?"

She held the necklace up in front of the crowd. It sparkled and glittered in the bright sun.

"The diamonds may not be real, but they are very pretty," Mrs. Peters said.

42

She began to read the bids that people had written on pieces of paper. "Ten dollars from Mrs. Dolan," she read.

That seemed like a lot of money to Molly.

"Twenty-five dollars from Joe Smithly," said Mrs. Peters.

Everyone cheered.

"Wow," said Lisa. "He must be rich."

Mrs. Peters kept reading off numbers and names. There were many bids in the box. Then all of a sudden she looked very surprised. "One thousand dollars!" she called.

"Ooh, aah," everyone said.

Who would bid one thousand dollars at a rummage sale?

The Pee Wee Scouts looked around.

"It's not my mom," said Lisa. "She doesn't have that much money."

"My mom does," said Rachel. "My dad's a dentist."

Rachel was always bragging about her dad, thought Molly.

The Pee Wees ignored Rachel.

"It must be a movie star," said Sonny.

Finally Mrs. Peters read the name on the paper. "Mrs. Noble," she said.

The Scouts looked all around. They tried to see if Mrs. Noble looked like a movie star.

"She'll have lots of makeup on her face," whispered Sonny.

"And gold rings on her fingers," said Tracy.

"Here I am!" called out a lady at the back of the crowd. "I'm Mrs. Noble."

But this lady did not have makeup on.

She did not wear gold rings. She had jeans on. And an old blue sweater.

"She's no movie star," scoffed Roger.

When she came closer, Tracy said, "Do you know who that is? That's the lady who gave us the necklace."

Molly looked. Rat's knees! Tracy was

45

right. Why would a lady pay one thousand dollars for her own necklace?

Mrs. Noble gave Mrs. Peters a check. Then she took the necklace. With a big smile on her face, she looked out into the crowd at Molly and Tracy and Mary Beth.

"When these nice girls came to my house," she said, "I was in such a hurry that I didn't realize I had given them my real diamond necklace."

Mrs. Peters's eyes opened wide. "Those were real diamonds in your wagon," she said.

"I knew that," said Molly.

"So did we," said Tracy and Mary Beth.

"The necklace is worth over ten thousand dollars," Mrs. Noble said with a smile.

Kevin whistled through his teeth.

"She is as rich as a movie star," said Tim. "Even if she isn't one."

"You could buy a house with ten thousand dollars. Or at least a sports car!" shouted Roger.

"It isn't just the money," said Mrs. Noble. "This necklace has been in my family a long time. I'm very glad to have it back. And I'm glad to donate this money to the animal shelter too."

Miss Penn went right up to the front of the crowd. "With this money," she said, "we can put in some new kennels with outdoor runs. Plus, we'll be able to take in more poor homeless dogs and cats for people to adopt. Thank you very much."

She shook Mrs. Noble's hand.

Mrs. Noble has pretty good rummage,

thought Molly. Thank goodness she and Mary Beth had gone along with bossy, drippy Tracy! If they hadn't, they would never have gone to Lake Street or to Mrs. Noble's house.

Maybe it wasn't so bad to be bossy after all.

At least when it's for a good cause.

# CHAPTER 8
# Leftover Puppy

That night the Pee Wee Scouts fell into bed. They were very hot. They were very tired. Molly was too tired even to eat supper. She slept like a rock.

But the next morning there was work to be done.

The Scouts rushed over to Mrs. Peters's house when they got up.

"I'll rake!" shouted Roger.

"I'll clean the garage," said Molly.

"I'll help Molly," said Mary Beth.

50

Sonny and I will pack up the leftover
rummage,"said Tim.

"Yeah," said Sonny. "We'll do it together."

All of the Scouts pitched in to help.

"Many hands make light work, my mom says," said Rachel.

By noon the yard was swept and cleaned.

Mrs. Peters poured some lemonade. It was another hot day.

"Yum," said Molly. She rubbed her stomach.

"Now," said Mrs. Peters, sitting down at the picnic table. "I want to congratulate Troop 23. You brought lots of money to the animal shelter. You brought more than any other Scout troop. But the best thing is, you all worked very hard. You did what Pee Wee Scouts should do. You helped others."

Molly was proud. She felt like bursting her buttons. Being a Scout made her feel good. Even if she didn't get a badge for it.

"We have only one thing to take care of," said Mrs. Peters.

"I know!" shouted Kevin. "The left-over puppy!"

The Pee Wees all looked at the one cage beside the driveway. Next to the cage sat one leftover puppy. All the others had been sold. Mrs. Peters had fed him and kept him in her house overnight.

Sonny brought the puppy some fresh water.

He patted him on the head.

Sonny was not afraid of puppies.

Only large dogs.

"We can't send him back," said Molly.

"Mrs. Peters, do we have to send this puppy back to the pound?" asked Tim.

"Well," said Mrs. Peters, pouring more lemonade for the Scouts, "we could use a mascot for Troop 23."

"Where would he live?" asked Molly, hoping it would be her house.

"We'll have to see if your mothers

would take turns keeping him," replied Mrs. Peters.

Tracy looked doubtful. She sneezed, loudly.

"Not Tracy's mom," added Mrs. Peters.

"Yeah!" the Scouts cheered. They all wanted a Pee Wee mascot. He was black with white feet. All the mothers will want him, thought Molly.

"Let's call him Spot," said Lisa.

"There are lots of better names than Spot," scoffed Rachel.

Lisa looked hurt.

"I like Paws," said Tracy.

"King," said Roger.

"Prince," said Kevin.

Mrs. Peters frowned. "Those are all good names," she said. "But if we do keep him, I think we should call him Lucky because he was lucky to be at a sale to help pets."

Troop 23 clapped loudly.

Some of the boys whistled.

Lucky was the best name for a maybe-mascot.

"This week," said Mrs. Peters, "I will call your mothers. If they agree to take turns keeping Lucky, we will have a mascot. I will let you know at our next meeting."

The Pee Wees groaned. It was a long time to wait.

Roger snapped a leash on Lucky's collar and took him for a run. Then everyone petted him. He tried to lick their hands. He wagged his tail.

"Lucky just has to be our mascot," said Mary Beth.

"He'll be a spoiled one," said Mrs. Peters, smiling.

"Why will he spoil?" said Tracy. She frowned.

The Scouts laughed.

"I mean he will get too much attention," said Mrs. Peters. "Not spoil like
food. If we keep him," she added.

Even though it was not a meeting, the
Scouts joined hands and sang their Scout

song. Then they said their Pee Wee Scout pledge.

Mrs. Peters looked pleased. Her troop had worked hard.

Harder than any other troop.

"Next week we will have new badges for you," she said.

The Scouts cheered at the news. They gave Lucky one last hug, and started home.

Molly felt good all over. They had worked hard. They would get new badges. They had helped homeless animals.

And maybe, just maybe, they would get a troop mascot.

# CHAPTER 9

# Mrs. Peters's Surprise

At last it was time for another meeting of the Pee Wees. Molly was eager to find out if the other mothers would agree to keep Lucky. Her mother had said yes.

Molly was excited about something else too. The Scouts had a surprise for Mrs. Peters.

During the week they had decided to give Mrs. Peters an end-of-the-summer thank-you party. Mrs. Peters had worked hard too.

Molly's mother made a huge cake.

Molly made a dog out of colored icing for the top. She gave the dog white paws. And a blue ribbon around his neck. A tag on the ribbon said LUCKY in little letters.

Sonny's mother sent potato salad from the deli. "Because she works," said Sonny proudly. "Otherwise she would have made it herself, she said."

Rachel's mother made little bitty sandwiches in the shape of dogs and cats. They had cream cheese and olives in them. Some had anchovies.

"Yuck," said Roger when he tasted one. He spit the anchovy out.

Rachel sighed. "My mother said she thought that might happen," Rachel told them. "She said some children might not know what anchovies were, if they didn't go to parties often."

Roger stuck out his tongue at her. He

brought hot dogs. His mother called them perfectly good-tasting hot dogs.

Tracy brought soda pop. "Allergy-free," she said. "It has no preservatives in it."

The Pee Wees couldn't wait to surprise Mrs. Peters. They snuck the food in the back door while some of the Pee Wees went to the front.

They tied balloons to the chairs.

They put the food on the table.

When Mrs. Peters came into the kitchen, they all yelled, "SURPRISE!"

Tiny and Lucky both began to bark.

"How exciting!" cried Mrs. Peters. "Oh, my goodness! What a nice way to end the dog days of August."

"Dog days?" said Kevin.

"The end-of-summer days in August are called dog days," Mrs. Peters explained. "When there is green algae on the lake and you can't swim."

Lucky howled at her words. Owoooo!

"We have our own dog days," said Molly. "We have had dog days the whole Help-a-Pet month!"

Everyone laughed and got in line behind Mrs. Peters for food.

Then their leader had badges to give out to the Scouts for working so hard at the rummage sale to help a pet. The Pee Wees pinned them on their shirts.

"Our troop surely helped pets more than any other troop!" said Mrs. Peters proudly.

The Scouts could not wait any longer.

"Do we have a mascot?" shouted Roger.

"Can we keep Lucky?" asked Molly.

Mrs. Peters smiled. The Scouts did not move.

"Yes!" she said. "There were enough mothers who could take turns keeping Lucky. So he is our new mascot."

Lucky barked a high puppy bark. Yip! Yip!

Tiny barked a low bark. Arf! Arf!

And Troop 23 cheered loudly. "Yeah!" they shouted. "He is ours!"

"And now," Mrs. Peters went on, "I have another little surprise for you."

The Scouts looked up at their leader.

What kind of a surprise? Molly wondered.

They had their new badges.

They had a Scout mascot.

What kind of a surprise could it be?

The Pee Wees sat on the floor in a big circle. Mrs. Peters sat in a chair. She smiled at the Scouts. Then she said, "My surprise is some big news. I am going to have a little Pee Wee Scout of my own. In a few months I am going to have a baby!"

The Pee Wees were very quiet. Molly

felt shocked. She had never thought of Mrs. Peters with a baby of her own. She was their Scout leader. She wasn't a mother.

Some of the Pee Wees looked at each other.

We should say we are happy, thought Molly. But instead Molly wanted to say, Will you still be our leader?

No one said anything. They just sat and looked at Mrs. Peters.

Then Roger whispered to Molly, "Babies can't be Scouts."

"I know you are all surprised," Mrs. Peters went on. "But I will still be your Scout leader. Our troop will still meet here every Tuesday. We will just have one more little Scout at our meetings."

"Yeah!" shouted Molly.

Then all the Pee Wees cheered.

The boys ran up and shook Mrs. Peters's hand. The girls gave her little hugs.

Then, when Mr. Peters came home, they cheered for him too.

A baby might be fun, thought Molly. She didn't have any little brothers or sisters.

"Maybe we can take it for a walk in a stroller," said Mary Beth.

Mary Beth was very motherly, thought Molly.

"My mom will buy it a real cute dress if it's a girl," said Rachel.

"I hope it doesn't have allergies," said Tracy, wiping her nose.

It was time for the surprise party to end.

They had come to give Mrs. Peters a surprise. And instead, she gave one to them!

The Pee Wees got into a circle. They held hands.

First they said the Pee Wee Scout pledge together. Then they sang the Pee Wee Scout song.

Suddenly Molly felt a good feeling in the bottom of her stomach. It felt like her birthday or Christmas. But it wasn't.

"Rat's knees!" she said. "I love Pee Wee Scouts!"

♪ ♪ Pee Wee Scout Song ♪ ♪

(to the tune of
"Old MacDonald Had a Farm")

Scouts are helpers, Scouts have fun,
Pee Wee, Pee Wee Scouts!
We sing and play when work is done,
Pee Wee, Pee Wee Scouts!

With a good deed here,
And an errand there,
Here a hand, there a hand,
Everywhere a good hand.

Scouts are helpers, Scouts have fun,
Pee Wee, Pee Wee Scouts!

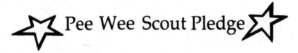 Pee Wee Scout Pledge

We love our country
And our home,
Our school and neighbors too.

As Pee Wee Scouts
We pledge our best
In everything we do.